THROUGH
My Eyes

THROUGH
My Eyes

Carol J. Allen

ReadersMagnet, LLC

Dedication

I dedicate this book to my husband of thirty years this year; William H. Allen.

Without his encouragement and help it could never have happened. We did it together.

As one to another:

The lord directed me to you,

At first I thought, how can this be!

But, over the years I've found the truth

That part of **you,** was part of **me.**

Appreciation

I give thanks to all the people in the book that gave me permission to write about them or use their name.

Some stories were true, some fiction and some a combination of both.

I especially thank God for my talent and the encouragement around me.

Author's Notes

Over the years many things have happened in my life. They remain vivid even today. Each incident is a story written in memories recalled, or at the time of the event. Even the poems express my thoughts and inspired me to share those thoughts with an interpretation that shows the influence people had on my life.

This book is only a small portion of what I have gathered over the years. They are meant to make the reader laugh and cry with me. I hope you enjoy it.

Contents

SECTION I
CHRISTIAN

God's Love Revealed

We are here but for a day

Material things are but pleasures along the way

What gift has been given by God my friend

What gift did He lend you to spend!

What plan does He have for you in this life!

To warrant the gifts He put in your care

Do you say "I love you (Abba) Father"!

Then go on your way

Or do you bask in His word

And talk to him every day.

You were designed for His perfect plan

Relax, submit and take Jesus by the hand.

One doesn't have to look very far

The Holy Spirit is in you wherever you are

Oh what a delight it will be

To set our crown at the Fathers feet

By walking in His word and loving embrace

As we carry out His desires

For the short walk in this place.

You Can't Steal My Joy

You can knock me down

You can steel my car

You can take my job

And sit on my pride

But you can't steal my joy

For that comes from the Lord.

You can slander my name

You can take my fame

You can throw stones

You can take my home

But you can't take my joy

For that comes from the Lord.

You can make me ill

You can sway my friends

You can shatter my dreams

You can do anything

But you can't take my joy

For that comes from the Lord.

Glory and the Fire

Before:

What is that you say?

Am I saved you ask!

<u>Glory and the fire</u> will show the way!

Will you come and see, you ask!

I'll just see, if

<u>Glory and the fire</u> can convince someone like me.

After:

I feel something in this place,

I must hurry to be saved in all due haste.

Lord, I didn't know the way to go

Until I saw this revealing show.

This is real - how filled I feel,

Tell me Lord, what is your will?

Heavens Blessings

Chorus:

I will yield, obey and give my life to Jesus

I will expect, react and watch the blessings grow

I will respond, yes respond to the Holy Spirit

And praise the Lord for all that I have.

Verse: 1

I will yield like Saul on the road to Damascus

For I am as ready as he

In faith, just obey, as my Lord clears the way

And I flow with the spirit every day.

Verse: 2

I will expect to receive even in adversity

For my strength comes from the Lord

I will react when He calls to all that He asks

For the joy of the Lord is my strength.

Verse: 3

I will respond to His work and follow His plan

The plan He made just for me

The Holy Spirit will guide me as He grows inside me

All in the strength of His word.

Once Upon a Time

At first a child so sweet and soft

Then rebellion breathed from the dark

Tragedy followed as it always does

Plunging my heart into deep pain and dispair.

But even in the deep, a door opens up

To reveal a glowing light from above

Just when I thought nothing was left

God pulled me out of that pit of death.

He cleaned my body and healed my wounds

He gave me new purpose and life

With his word as my guide

He gave me a mate with wisdom and drive

Then sent us both forward to plant his seed.

He said, "When you were down, I picked you up

When you were wounded, I healed you

Now hear my command and follow me for

The kingdom belongs to those who take my hand

Yesterday's gone and today is here and

Tomorrow holds the treasures for those who follow

Without fear, MY WAY".

Lord Jesus, I Love You

Lord Jesus I Love you but I can't count the ways

You're the maker of my dreams,

the love with in my soul

You're in me and on me, all around me oh Lord

And I love you but, I can't count the ways

You're in the air I breath, the life I live

You're in the songs I sing, the light for all to see

I want the world to know that you're a part of me

But, if you were to ask me Lord

I'd say I love you but, I can't count the ways.

Shoo Shoo Devil

Shoo, Shoo devil

You can't come in.

Shoo, Shoo devil

Here you can not win.

This is the place that Jesus made

This is the place where souls are saved

This is the place where love is found

And where the Holy Spirit walks around

So, Shoo Shoo devil you can't come in.

Tounges

What manner of speech

That's coming from my mouth!

My head cannot comprehend

Nor even figure out

What manner of speech is this?

My mouth utters sounds that

Leave my soul a gasp

Bubbling out just any time

Be it in church, home, work, or

Tucked in bed so snug.

Who woke me?

It must be the Holy Spirit

Talking to my Jesus in the middle of the night.

10-19-1998
Pastor Hallam,
I wish to share God's revelation to me through your teaching––

Jubilee Time

I sang to my God in heaven above,

You've sent me your bounty and love.

Give me the wisdom that I might know,

And thereby proceed to steadily grow.

With joy in my heart and excited anticipation,

I look for your bounty and your wisdom.

This was His reply:

I have given you a place where the

Holy Spirit runs free,

(ALCC)

Jesus being the corner stone, can you not see!

A pastor obedient to my word,

(Hallam)

Be ye alas obedient to the place

I have called you to be.

From your pastor, be taught, for soon you will see.

All that I have will be yours as you grow,

There will be peace, wisdom,

joy and bounty in all that you do,

As my grace fills your life in love from me to you.

P.S. Pastor

As poetry swirls around in your mind, it is a joy to be reminded that God doesn't just have one gift per person, but many gifts spreading across the land for all His children, like the beauty of a newly fallen snow.

ALCC = Abundant Life Christian Center

Born Again

I have the Lord in my life, oh yes

I have the Lord in my life

I praise Him every day in everything I say for

I have the Lord in my life.

I have His song in my heart, oh yes

I have His song in my heart

And I'll sing of Him every day

Forever come what may.

For I have His song in my heart.

Sing praises to His name

And rise to the glory of His light.

Sing Praises of His greatness

As you sleep in His peace tonight.

SECTION II
THOUGHTFUL

Warning

While the dog is away the cat will play

While the cat is away the mouse will play

So my advise today, if you're away

Best hurry back home without delay

And that's all I'm going to say.

The Adventurous Spirit

The adventurous ones grow in fame and fortune

To me there is no doubt

If you don't want to be left behind

It's time you figured that out.

Look at Christopher Columbus, don't you agree

He was an example for all to see

For his adventurous spirit, yes siree

You'll find him in the books of history.

How about the presidents throughout time

Each made decisions over the land

They were important you will find

We witnessed their works fist hand.

Think of what you could do my friend

How about a poem now and then

Or maybe a painting that withstands time

A painting to express like a poem that rhymes.

My Meadow

Over in a meadow tall and green

Lying in the middle, not to be seen.

The clouds slowly passing by

Each clearly separate from a blue, blue sky.

No honking horns, no noisy din

No one watching, no one can

No hurry, no rush, only to be aware

Of the breeze gently blowing through the air.

Rustling leaves caressing me so

Please don't tell anyone you know

Drifting peacefully off to sleep

Thinking this is a place I'd love to keep.

We Give Thanks

Pilgrims landed at Plymouth rock

And prayed to god for what they got

A feast, a harvest of plenty, confident

This would be the first of many.

Struggling hard through winter cold

Through it all remaining strong and bold

Established for all a freedom grand

In America – the promised land.

Legacy

What happened to all the ambition

That disappeared with the evolution of time?

What happened to all the desires

That youth conspires to find?

Yesterday has come and gone

Today is but a fleeting glance

Tomorrow is too far away

And I seem to get lost in the games of chance.

What will I leave behind to encourage a child?

In all of this world that life is worth while

This is the answer not nearly profound

To love one another is the best common ground.

Take the God given talents you have at hand

And spread them generously across the land.

Rich/Poor

Here was a good way to make money I'm told

Everyone's been doing it successfully

Before they grow old

Everyone in the whole wide world

Everyone except me when I gave it a whirl.

If anything can go wrong along the way

It always happens to me, needless to say

Why can't I be like everyone else

To have just some fame and fortune would certainly

help.

Life

Life is what you make it they say

Of course it depends on influence along the way

Some you might consider good and some bad

And how much of each you've had.

How you respond would indeed come into play

For you need to handle them in just the right way.

Your age could determine if you win or lose

Depending on whether it was big or small in your mind

Would it affect your future or could you leave it behind.

Wow, I never thought about it before

Now life could be complicated for ever more.

I Just Can't Say No

Do I look secure to you?

Nothing could be further from the truth

Yet the tasks you ask me to do

Would have been easier in my youth,

Even so I just can't say "NO".

I practice "No, No, No"

But somehow I just go go go.

It doesn't seem to matter how difficult the chore

When you want it done, you'll come knocking at my door.

Somehow I just can't say no.

When I see you coming,

I could lock myself inside

But there seems no place for me to hide.

The doorbell rings, the horn honks, the telephone rings

It's still the same old song I always sing

I just can't say no.

After I'm gone, who will take my place

As I escape in time and space.

Will the one you choose to take my place

Do all you ask with style and grace?

SECTION III
FACTUAL

Hurricane Ike

In the big city of Houston where I live

Hurricane IKE came blowing in.

Great devastation began.

Trees fell, shingles flew, windows broke,

Debris grew, electricity was gone.

Darkness prolonged and then the water came

Flooding areas, adding to pain but,

When it was gone, some blessings came.

Neighbors helped neighbors and I did the same,

Cleaning and mending it all was our aim.

Neighbors talked while they worked, I'm so glad.

No going to work, no computers, no TV, no hot water

Gas lines for cars galore, no air and

Just cooking on the grill, flash lights and candles.

Needless to say, a whole lot more.

What do you do when there's no TV?

Why, visit the neighbors, that's for me.

Fat City

All of my life I've been skinny

Skinny as a pin

Then, when I turned fifty

Fat came pouring in.

No matter how I diet or how much I do not eat

Fat plagues my belly, arms, legs, and seat.

I don't need an enemy from North, East, West or South

My enemy is fat and I just can't get fat out.

It gathers everywhere inside and

shows on every inch of hide.

So everyone in the world can see

What cloths can't even hide.

If I Had My Druthers

If I had my druthers

I'd never see a storm

And no one in this world

Could do another harm

If I had my druthers

Peace would reign everywhere

And no one would want to harm another

Not a single hair

If I had my druthers

There would never be an earthquake

The only way the earth would move

Is with a shovel and a rake

If I had my druthers

No one would ever get sick

No one could hit an animal

With any kind of stick

If I had my druthers

There would be food enough to go around

It would pop everywhere from the ground

Parents would never separate

Until they reached the heavenly gate

If I had my druthers.

This poem also appears in "The Best Poems and Poets of 2007"
buy The International Library of Poetry in 2008

Busy Busy

Up in the morning

Out on the job

No time to waste

No time to hobnob.

First work on the job

Then errands to run

Supper to make

House to clean

Everyday the same routine.

Head for the bed

Turn down the phone

It can be thankfully said

HURAH! for anytime of my own.

Foolish Girl

Sixteen and married, many a teenagers dream

But, dreams don't always come true

Four children and left all alone

This is a warning from me to you.

Heart aches by the numbers, a life time to atone.

First, a girl like a rose growing wild

Now sixteen and just like me

The same heartaches she will see.

Second a boy, my pride and joy

But like his father, love couldn't keep him home

Heartaches by the number and more to know.

Then came a boy, different from the rest

All that I hoped a child could be

Still, one day he too would say, "It's time for me to go

my way".

Last but not least a daughter

With a body full blown and a mind of her own

She would not be left behind!

I pray she will grow wise with the passing of time.

When they are all gone

And the door has closed behind

I pray the Lord be merciful and kind

And true love they will find.

Love In The Work Place

Here is to second shift tried and true

From all of my being I dedicate this ode to you

A well rounded cooperative hard working group

And if you read this poem, you'll get the whole scoop.

Avid and eager they come in each day

All of their abilities ready to put into play

In anticipation they listen to goals

Ready to plug up any troublesome holes.

Each taking station where they'll do the most good

Every job is important to reach the great heights

That show how valuable the team is on nights.

So bring your goals and your obstacles too

The night shift will beat them with all their qualities

That they will do.

Note: This poem was written by me in 1980 when I was the foreman of the plant where I worked, on the night shift and was published in the company paper.

A Mission to the Philippines

Two thousand was God's approved time

For a mission trip to the Philippines, I find

We dyed our hair black that we might blend in

Something like our black haired, dark skinned friends.

But, our hair remained light and our skin was too white.

God said "You'll accomplish more by far

If you go as you are.

We traveled through Manila, Zamboanga and Cebu

With our Philippine friend, then traveled home again.

He had opened the door and guided us each day.

Our mission was accomplished and we did it God's way.

SECTION IV
SERIOUS

Death of a Lady

On a porch in a rocker sits a lady

She is old and her hair has turned to grey

She just sits there alone in that rocker

And she rocks her life away.

Doesn't anybody care about this lady!

Doesn't anybody want to know!

Where are the children of her youth!

Where did all her loved ones go!

Look at the smile on her face

See the tears in her eyes

Down within, the flames burn low

I think this lady will die.

See the sunset in the west

A blanket of darkness oe'er her pressed

And with the darkness the flame went out.

It must have been the hand of God

That came to take her home

He took her home to be with Him

Now she'll never be alone.

Also available in the book of "Collected Whispers"
By the International Library of Poetry in 2008

Love is Not Easy

It isn't easy to be in love with you

Nor easy to show you that I do

It's not easy to change my way of life

Nor is it easy to walk in your light.

Come and take my hand

We'll travel oe'er God's land

I know He understands

For Him it's always easy.

Someday when we'll have to part

That's the day it will break my heart

And though we'll have to say good-by

All God's children will meet one day in the sky.

Our love won't be easy,

It's never easy

He never said it would be easy

But, I'm willin.

You Say You Love Me

You say you love me

Well that's all right

You say you want me to be your wife

Before I agree, there is something I must say

So I'll say it just this way.

I need individuality and

I need my own personality

I want people to like me for myself

And not just a dolly on your shelf.

I need – room – room to breathe

Just a little bit of space to call my own

Then you will surely find

I will love you until the end of time

If you will only give me room to breathe.

Intimidation

You know something I doesn't know?

Tell me, tell me, so I too can grow

Or are you afraid to teach me or make me wise?

Would I be a threat in your eyes?

That for me to learn would take your roll?

Remember how Saul felt about David?

This story is told in our Bible so sacred.

Maybe we could share a thing or two

I know that God would want us to

He has placed us together for a season

Teaching each other could be a part of the reason.

Jealousy and intimidation are a sin, but humility

Will bring forgiveness over and over again.

We all have talents we were given to share,

To spread them here and to spread them there.

If you turn me down, I'll just move to another

And, we'll never get to really know each other.

Our talents together, could have greater things made

But instead, they become not color but shadows of

shade.

Children of Disobediance

Disobedience runs rampant over the land

Fear and heartbreak close at hand

No one seems concerned and none understand

These are our leaders of tomorrow

Self willed and cruel predict pain and sorrow.

Who cares if mother is being abused

Or dad would kill before he would loose

Who cares if baby watches the scene

And as he grows up repeats what he's seen.

Spoil the child, let him do what he wants

Disrespect is acceptable as seen every day

Question a parent and this they will say

We can't discipline them and there's no other way.

How did we get in such a state?

Do you think there's a chance or is it too late?

To change what is happening to cause such a fate

And having one parent is definitely not great.

Feuding and fighting is apart of it all

Killing for religion an excuse to brawl

Discarding each other when newness wares off

Helps teach little children it's not necessary to bond

So, pain and sorrow marches on.

SECTION V
HUMOROUS

Sin

Here is sin, there is sin, everywhere is sin

The world is full of sin

Who opened that door and let the nasty devil in?

It wasn't me you can plainly see

So it must have been you, it seems to me

Why, you know I'm as innocent as I can be

I'd never kick your dog or step on a baby frog

And never sass my Mom, at least not face to face

Nor would I trip the one next to me if we had a foot race

Or flatten the neighbors bicycle tire

Or play with matches and set the garage on fire

Along with a million other things that have been done

I'd guess it was the devil just having a little fun.

Forget Nots

I can remember to pay the bills

But not where I put them, if you will

And, I can remember to make an appointment

But not the date or where it went.

My drawers are filled with pills of all kinds

But what they are for is not written I find

And my bookshelf is empty due to books loaned out

To whom they were loaned, I can't figure out.

My mother had said to make a note to help

But inadvertently I'll throw the note out

Here a note, there a note, everywhere a note

Now which one and where is the right one I wrote?

I'll call a friend with something to say

But first, to be polite, I'll let her talk away

Then she'll ask, "And why did you call?"

I'll have forgotten so the answer is, "Nothing at all".

Put it on a bulletin board you say?

Then what do I do when I'm away?

Tell me, tell me what would you do?

Hurry to answer, that is if you can find me too.

Testing

Here was a boy friend my parents should like

As soon as they met him, I knew I was right

<u>Maybe</u> we could test the waters by

living together for a while

Make sure there would be no divorce

after a walk down the aisle

My parents were opposed you could plainly see

Reluctantly unhappy they promised to be

Silent long enough to watchfully see

But then came his birthday

And much to our surprise

Came his birthday cake

With a bride and groom to try on for size.

Help Me

Today was especially frustrating at work

Nothing went smooth, all things seem to jerk

Upon entering the house, one could easily see

A husband quietly watching TV.

Gently sliding onto his lap

Arms around his neck, a kiss and a pat

I said, "Honey, how about just a little rest!"

He looked as though he'd been given a test

He responded, "Sure but, who will you get

To make up our supper and turn down our bed?"

L-O-V-E Love

There's a love bug attached to an arrow

And the arrow is drawn with a bow

And the bow was held by a man

All was controlled by his hand

Sing'n dum diddie dum dum,

dum didie dum dum

Sing'n dum diddie dum dum

That's L-O-V-E love.

Now the man pulled back his bow

And the bow let go of the arrow

The arrow soared through the air

And the arrow hit me, you know where.

Singin dum diddie dum dum,

Dum diddie dum dum

Singin sum diddie dum dum

That's L-O-V-E love

Yes, his hand let go of the bow

And the bow let go of the arrow

The arrow soared through the air

The love bug bit me, right there.

Count To Three – No Siree

Behave yourself, I'll count to three

Then you'll be sorry, you will see

One ___ Two ___ Three

How absurd, don't you agree?

Everyone knows they'll wait till three

You can bet your last dollar, yes siree.

Why not count to two, the better thing to do

Less time to test if what you say is true

Far easier on the nerves by far, for you.

Better yet, let's count to one

Now the process has already begun

And quick as a wink, it's already done.

Children go by your lead every day

Why test their obedience in such an absurd way?

A habit they'll form throughout life

And don't you suppose it could cause consequences or

strife?

What do they do with the rules put forth in our world?

There's no one, two, three, or you'll be sorry, you'll see.

You don't want this to happen, don't you agree?

So teach them the rules that are meant to be

For in this world, there maybe no second chance

Believe me my friend, they'll thank you for a life

enhanced.

Black and White

What if everything was black or white!

Like, now it's day or now it's night.

And shapes would be the only way

To tell what flowers were in bloom today.

The leaves would only be black, that's all

So we could not tell our summer from our fall.

We would know it's winter simply because

There would be no leaves on trees, for us.

It would be easy to tell and know the reason why

The sun in the morning would blend with the sky

And we would know the moon by the black of night

For out of the darkness it would shine so bright.

The world as a whole, would be an uninspiring sight

If everything was just plain old black or white.

Hurrah for color and every blend

So all of these thoughts won't come again.

SECTION VI
SHORT STORIES

A Bumpy Weekend with Donna the Tomboy

Donna or "Butch", as she was called by everyone except her mother, launched an attack on the alarm clock buzzing in her ear. It was on the night stand beside her bed. Her chubby body hit the floor with a thud. Mountains of waist length black hair hid her broad shoulders and chubby, freckled face from sight. Beneath thick bangs peered two green eyes sparkling with excitement. This is gonna be a great weekend Donna thought to herself as she headed toward the bathroom. A smile from ear to ear, revealed thoughts of sheer delight at convincing her Mom to let her spend Friday and Saturday with Mr. and Mrs. Henry, the neighbors two doors away from their house. This way she would get out of helping with the cooking and cleaning for Sunday's family reunion.

Mr. and Mrs. Henry had a snooty twelve year old daughter they named Lucy and a son who was so cool at about fourteen, Donna guessed. His name was Charley. Charley would let her play football with him and his friends and they would look at comic books he collected and we even traded some baseball cards. Wow, it made Donna tingle all over just thinking about it.

In the bathroom Donna did her usual splish, splash on the face, tied her hair back and brushed the surface. She scrubbed the teeth rigorously, checked her appearance and headed for the kitchen. There she poured a bowl of her favorite cereal and began to eat by heaping teaspoonful. Suddenly Mom appeared with both hands on her hips and a scowl on her face.

"What's up Mom?"

"You know very well what's up. Go back in the bathroom and clean up your mess."

In spite of the day starting a little ruff, school went well and freedom was in sight. Donna entered the house with her usual flair, slamming the door behind her.

"Where's everybody? I'm home."

From the bedroom her Mother called, "In here cleaning, Donna."

"Just checking in Mom. I'm gone, ok?"

"Be good, and change your clothes before you go."

"I will, bye Mom," she shouted as the door slammed behind her.

Lucy watched Donna coming down the sidewalk toward her and all she could think of is that Donna had less grace than her dog greeting the mailman. How gross, Lucy thought sullenly.

Before Donna could even get close to Lucy she shouted, "Let's hurry to your house. I'm hungry. Your mom might have something good to eat."

Lucy ignored her, "Mom is taking us to the show tomorrow, Butch. Mom's not home yet so we have the house all to ourselves," she teased.

"What cha mean" Where's Charley?"

"Charley is off with dad on a fishing trip this weekend, again. Dad picked him up right from school."

What a revolting development this is, thought Donna. Just my luck.

The weekend was boring without football and Charley. Am I glad it's Sunday thought Donna as she entered the house slamming the door behind her. It's good to be home. One more minute with Lucy would be more than I could take, Donna thought. Donna's nose caught the aroma of fresh baked cookies. Taking a deep breath, she followed that irresistible aroma coming from the kitchen. Just glad to be home, she gave her Mom a fast hug and headed out the door to find a football game. Oops, just one more cookie and I'm gone. Donna spun around with surprising grace and agility for a stocky bowlegged ten-year-old and disappeared before her Mom could repeat all the instructions for this special Sunday, that she did not want to hear.

Donna, Friend or Foe

Today was our family reunion, finally. I have been waiting since last year for it to come again. My name is Donna and my nose can smell a fresh baked cookie from anywhere in the house. That smell is like an invisible hand leading me to the kitchen and I am its prisoner.

Let me describe myself to you. I'm four and a half feet tall and very fast. Why I'm as fast as a cork popping from a wine bottle. Mom says my hair is always a mess at waist length and black as coal. It covers my shoulders and that's good because my shoulders are very big. I'm, a little bit chubby and my face is covered with freckles. Beneath my thick bangs are two green eyes, if you can see them. I know they sparkle with excitement when company is coming because my mother said so.

"Wow, Mom, this is gonna be a big one, I can feel it in my bones. We're gonna have wall to wall people. I suppose you want me to entertain them, huh! I just need one more cookie to test."

"First, get that sloppy flannel shirt off and put on some clean jeans. As soon as you change, I want you to find your sister and both of you report back to the kitchen to help clean up the dirty kitchen cooking has caused and no more cookies."

"Yuk, dishes."

"Donna, don't start pouting and lower those bushy eyebrows at me. Throwing yourself on that chair with that attitude won't get you anywhere either."

"Why can't Joy do the dishes while I entertain? No one would even miss her and besides, she's the oldest and dishes go with her personality. I know where to find her; she's either behind the couch or chair sleeping or in the back of the closet reading a dumb old book. Nobody likes a bookworm and besides that she doesn't like anybody either..."

"Donna, I don't want to hear another word and stop eating the cookies. If you treated her better, she probably wouldn't be that way. If the other kids saw you treat her better, so would they because, they follow everything you do."

"It's a good thing I don't or she would ruin my reputation. Take yesterday for example, I took her with me to play baseball and neither team wanted her. We decided by walking the bat, now half the kids are mad at me. The half that lost, of course."

Relatives had started to arrive and I could hear them talking and laughing as they greeted each other with hugs and kisses, ready to pour out every little detail of the last year. Now that could be stopped from happening with a lot of good entertainment.

I'm thinking I can make it to the doorway in three easy hops, just like a frog, or maybe a toad would be more like it. I'll bet I can even do it gracefully and quickly. Do your thing, Donna. Atta girl I knew you could do it... "Come on Mom, let me go and I'll show you what I can do".

"The faster you find your sister and get those dishes done, the sooner our relatives will have the pleasure of your company. Don't forget to change your clothes and comb your hair before you let anyone see you."

"You do know you are asking me to take off my favorite football clothes and that the guys are picking me up later this afternoon to play ball. Why, you wouldn't want me to mess up my good clothes, would you?"

"Don't you ever play with the girls?"

"Oh sure, but not the same way or at the same time. I have to keep them separated. Trust me Mom; I know what I'm doing."

"Donna, leave those cookies alone," said her mom as Donna ran from the room with a cookie in each hand. Mom smiled knowing Donna was just like her father, a magnetic personality with boundless energy that drew in young and old. Making coffee for the second time, she visualized Donna as the first woman president, a whip in one hand and waving with the other while the public willingly bowed in reverence. She wondered if people would still call her wild daughter "Butch" when she was grown.

———

When The Lights Go Out

Its bedtime and dark in my bedroom upstairs. To make matters worse, the light in the stairway was out. The bulb needed changing and only my dad could reach it and he needed a ladder.

Everyone knows the monsters come out when it's dark. We lived in this big old spooky house in the country. It must be haunted. I lay awake at night and listen to the creaks and groans. It reminds me of my grandpa, old and crooked. It never bothered me much until my brother Jimmy went to college because he would always carry me upstairs and tuck me into bed. I sure miss him, especially after dark. Jimmy would always wrestle and play with me. He calls me his wild and wooly sister. I love my brother. Jimmy tosses me on the bed with instructions to cover up and go to sleep before the monsters get me. At eight years old, it was too soon for him to leave me all alone, I wasn't ready.

More then once goose pimples stood out on my body as the chimes on the hall clock warned me, it was bedtime. It was then that I knew the monsters would come out playing on the stairs. I stood at the bottom, straining in the dark to see if they were out. Sure enough, shadows could be seen playing up and down the walls from the lights through the window half way up the stairs. A light breeze like movement from the ceiling fan drifted down and encircled me making a chill to the bone. How I hated those stairs when the light was out and Jimmy wasn't there to protect me from those monsters.

Taking a deep breath, I made a mad dash up the stairs. Half way up I stooped and flattened my back against the wall under the window. My heart was beating so fast, I thought it might burst into a million peaces any minute. The half way point and they hadn't got me yet. The trick was to make a lot of noise and scare them so they would get out of the way. The old switcheroo.

Darn, this is worse then going through the haunted house at the fair, where monsters jumped out at you and scared you half to death. It was fun there but not in your own house. Besides, you weren't alone at the fair, there were a bunch of other kids screaming too.

Ok, back to the nightmare at hand. Another mad dash and I hit the light just inside my bedroom door and the monsters were gone. Mom has tried to tell me that there is nothing in the dark that isn't there when the lights are on. She thinks I have a wild imagination, not so, she just doesn't understand about how monsters think. Quickly checking the closet and under the bed as well as under the covers to make sure there was no monsters lurking about, I hit the light switch and dashed across the room, jumped into bed, pulling the covers over me like a tent, leaving only a peep hole to breath.

Wow, I did all this without Jimmy. I said my prayers and drifted off to sleep, absolutely sure that covers were partly invented to help protect me from the monsters.

I had conquered those monsters all by myself and they better find someone else to bother because I'm too grown up to let them bother me now.

Nobody's Perfect

Buzzzzz, wack, damn that clock, I don't want to get up. Wait a minute Donna, you big dummy, it's Friday. Rise and shine. School will be over before you know it and you'll be spending the weekend at Kathy's. If it weren't for Kathy, there would be no way for me to be near her dreamy brother Charley. It's sure hard to get an invite out of her, I wonder if she knows how I feel about her brother. Nuts, no sense wishing he was my brother cause then things would not be the same. Why do I like Charley anyway! Well, let me see, he's the only one who would take the time to teach me how to play a good game of football like the pros do and not like some sissy. He's not afraid to tackle me or pounce on me and I have the bruises to prove it. Besides that, Charley smells good. He doesn't even have bad breath and he treats me like one of the guys.

Sure wish Mom would get some tooth powder like his instead of this old toothpaste we have. Charley's toothpaste comes in a can and he just sprinkles it on, now how cool is that!

Hope he doesn't know I use his toothpaste when I'm at his house.

Yipes! All this day dreaming is going to make me late for school. Maybe I can still get to the bathroom before anyone else does. What's in this can? By God, I think Mom did buy some toothpowder in a can. She must be reading my mind. A quick shower and then after a little splish splash and my teeth cleaned, once over with the comb and I'm out of here. Ok, wet the old toothbrush, sprinkle on the powder and into the mouth. Ug, what is this crap, it tastes awful. It sure doesn't taste like Charley's toothpaste. Where is my toothpaste? Man, that is some nasty stuff. Even my toothpaste isn't taking away the taste of that crap, maybe breakfast will.

One last look in the mirror. Boy, do you look sorry. Dull black hair ug, and your face looks like it's forever dirty and those freckles don't help. What about that big nose, it looks like a big bubble growing out of the middle of my face. Can't laugh at my Dad's nose, it looks just like mine. Now I'm getting in a bad mood.

If anyone calls me Butch today, I'm gonna give them a knuckle sandwich.

Humm, smells like cookies in the kitchen. Maybe Mom will let me have a couple to test. The smell is all over the kitchen but I don't see them anywhere.

Ok, who's hand is squeezing my head! "Oh, it's you Mom. What's up?"

"Young lady have you been into my deodorant in the bathroom?"

"Your what?"

"You heard me the first time. It's all over the bathroom."

I think I'm gonna be sick Mom. Make way for the toilet, I'm coming through.

"While your at it young lady, clean up your mess and be sure to be home early Saturday afternoon to help get ready for church on Sunday."

Yeah, yeah - aw nuts, I'm sure to be late for school after cleaning this mess.

School's out school's out, teacher let the fools out. "Come on Kathy, lets get to your house".

"Sure Donna, we can do whatever we want cause my brother and Dad went fishing for the weekend."

"Huh, he did? Gosh, what are we going to do now all by ourselves?"

"Mom is going to take us to the show and then she will drop you off at your house. She said we can even get popcorn."

Great I can hardly wait, I guess.

Holy Cow – What Happened?

Someone was nudging me out of my sleep. I opened one eye and in the dim light of morning, I could see it was my mother standing over me, shaking my shoulder. It was definitely not my brother who slept across the room.

"Wake up, wake up, I need to talk to you", she said.

"Gosh Mom, there is no school today, why did you wake me up?"

"Listen to me Donna I left a chicken thawing in the sink. The chicken is for supper but I won't get home from work early enough to fix it so, I need your help. Are you awake Donna? Donna are you awake? Do you hear me?"

"Yes, but I don't know how to fix a chicken Mom!"

"It is about time you started to learn to help around the house, after all you are fourteen years old and I really do need your help so, sit up and pay attention."

"Ok mom, what do I have to do", yawning and stretching to wake up.

"Scrub the chicken under the faucet and put it in the large pot filled with water, turn on the burner half way so it won't boil over and put the cover on, which you will find next to the pot.

Be sure to check the pot once in a while so it doesn't boil over. If the cover is dancing around on top of the pot, turn the burner down until it stops dancing. You can start cooking it about 5 p.m. When I get home at 6 p.m., I'll make dumplings."

"Ok Mom, seems easy enough, I think I can do that alright."

"Give me a kiss before I go and promise me you will not fight with your brother today."

"Ok Mom, I'll try not to. Just a few more minutes of sleep before I get up."

Wait a minute I could get that chicken ready right now and not have to turn on the stove until 5 p.m. Tippy toe down the stairs, Donna, so no one will wake up. There is the chicken in the sink alright. God, let me have your help with this dumb chicken, I pray. Ok, put the stopper in the hole and fill the sink with water. Now, let's see, where's the soap. Ah, the dish soap is right here so that must be what she wanted me to use. First swish the soap around for lots of suds, then in goes the chicken. Rub-a-dub dub, one chicken in the tub. Scrub it all over and let out the water. Now, it's a good idea to rinse off the soap I guess and into the pot it goes. Now, off to play football with Eric and John, down the road and if they are not up yet, I'll wake them up. If I have to get up so do they. Nuts, Jimmy isn't awake yet but that can be solved right now.

"Wake up Jimmy, before you end up on the floor. Time is wasting and I need to go and you need to go with me. Wake up."

The day sure went fast; it's almost 5 p.m., time to turn on the chick. I'll just change my muddy old cloths while waiting for the chicken to start cooking. Up the stairs and into the bathroom for a little scrub-a-dub on Donna before the chicken. Put on some clean clothes and away I go to check on the bird.

What's this, there's bubbles everywhere. I wonder if it is supposed to do that? Wow, right over the pot. I need something to catch and scoop off these bubbles. I'll just get another pot and a big spoon and scoop them into the pot, that way I can throw the bubbles in the sink. Where's the towel to clean this mess!

Thirty minutes later: They seem to be all gone just in time for the chick to finish cooking before mom gets home.

Mom, comes home and makes the dumplings. Soon supper is ready and everyone sits down to eat. Dad says the prayer and begins to dish out the food.

Jimmy takes the first bite, "Yuk, this tastes awful, Mom."

"Let me see," as Mom tastes the chicken. "Oh, my Donna, what did you do?'

"Nothing Mom that you didn't tell me to do. I guess I didn't get all of the soap out. It did bubble a lot while it was cooking."

"You did what! Donna, you were not supposed to use soap to wash it, just water."

Jimmy: "Any dummy knows that."

Mom: "It was an honest mistake so let's not dwell on it. We can eat our bread and vegetables and I'll cut us some of the leftover ham in the refrigerator."

Jimmy: "Hey Mom, why not make Donna eat the chicken!"

"I think Donna's been punished enough and she won't do that again will you! That was a hard lesson and we won't talk about it again. Now eat your food Jimmy."

Mom must have saw how my face was so red, the freckles probably could no longer be seen and my voice quivered from holding back the tears.

"I'm sorry Mom."

Sister, Sister

Donna had long, dark black flowing hair and dark creamy complexion but, a little on the chubby side. She had a great personality that drew people to her, like bees to honey. On the other hand, I was tiny, skinny and had long straggly dishwater blonde hair and a big nose that didn't look like it belonged to the rest of me. My personality was nothing to brag about either. I was shy and quiet. No one could tell we belonged to the same family as we walked down the street together.

One day Donna made plans to skip school with her friends. "Go to school and tell the teacher I'm sick, Karen," she instructed.

"NO, let me stay with you. I don't want to go to school by myself', I pleaded.

"Ah, we don't want you around, besides somebody has to tell the teacher I'm sick or she'll call Mom."

That was such a mean thing to say, that I started to cry. It didn't take much to make me cry.

"OK, OK, you can stay ya brat. If we get caught, you're gonna pay, watch and see."

We all just sat around at Donnas' friend's house and starred at each other.

"What ya wanna do?" Asked one of the girls.

"Lets play school", another volunteered.

How dumb, that's just what we did all day. We might as well have been in school.

There was a truant officer that checked on kids who didn't show up for school. Especially, when there were five of us missing all at the same time. Three of us were in the same fourth grade class and two were in the same fifth grade class with Mrs. Bowinski. She was tough and mean and she didn't like me anyway. They must have called Mom out of work when we didn't seem to be home. After all anything could have happened to us.

It was about one o'clock when mom came to the door. She banged on the door.

"Open this door right this minute," she shouted. "I know you're in there".

It was Donna that opened the door.

"Get your coats. You and your sister are going to school", she spoke with a stem voice.

Silently we put on our coats and I looked over at Donna. There was no doubt she was going to whop me first chance she got. Mom didn't say anything all the way to school. The three of us walked to my class first and Mom talked to the teacher, then she left me there continuing down the hall with Donna.

My teacher, Mrs. Bowinski, grabbed me by the arm and thrust me toward a seat in the third group where all the dummies sat. The rest of the day, she made nasty comments directed at me. From that day on, she made me an example of what happens to bad kids. Until now all my grades were as high as one could get in every class I'd been in. She never let up on me and I nearly flunked her class. Because of my past record, the school knew something was wrong and they passed me, in spite of the low grades I was suddenly getting. Good thing it was near the end of the school year. In the sixth grade, my grades went back to near perfect and Mrs. Bowinski was fired. It seems, I was not the only one she did that to.

Anyway, the kids found out what happened to me and felt sorry for me, all except Donna. She never did get any kind of punishment or at least none that I heard of. She probably convinced everyone it was my fault because, after all, I was the oldest. Besides, Donna did get even with a beating but, it didn't hurt any more than all the other beatings I took. The only good thing to say is, she wouldn't let anyone else hurt me. Donna considered me her personal punching bag.

As long as Donna could be the center of attention and I stayed in the back ground, we got along ok. I called it letting her be the big cheese.

When company came, Donna would sing dance, or even stand on her head if necessary and it worked out well because I would rather watch. Sometimes though, it did bother me that no one knew I was there until they were leaving and would ask where I was. They didn't see me sitting there all along.

Mom and Dad always said I wasn't pretty but I had brains. It would be a good time to gloat because she may have looks and personality but I had the brains. She was such a dummy. She only made passing grades and I made high grades. Being an honor student had its' good points. This allowed me to be on the service squad, movie squad, in the band, track team and future nurses and out of classes to do these things. All of this was sure to get me a big letter. All Donna managed to do was get on the volleyball team. What happened? It really hurt when the letters were given out for our achievements. She got a big one and I got a little one. How that could happen is beyond me?

"You didn't get that letter fairly," I wined.

"Yes I did," Donna said with a grin. "Can I help it if my typing teacher likes me so much she gave me more?"

It was bad enough being Donnas' shadow in everything else but not in the only thing to my credit. This means I had to think of a way to get back my rightful place as the brains. Since she out did me in the brains area, I had to out maneuver her in the brawn area. A plan was forming and it was about to take that smug look off of her face.

The plan was to get her mad. She didn't think well when she was mad. Donna would lower her head and come at you like a bull, butting her target in the stomach and the fight would be over. I swear she even snorted like a bull. Anyway this time there was a plan, just like a bull fighter fighting the bull, get it! The front porch was perfect because space was limited.

"Donna, come out on the porch, I have something to tell you. Now that you're here, I think you should know that you're a stupid, cheating, creep."

"Take that back or I'll cram it down your throat," Donna threatened.

"You and what army," I responded. "You make me sick. Everybody thinks you're so beautiful and nice but, you're just a sneaky slob and I should know cause we have to live together."

She was angry and ready, and I was scared. Her smile was gone and replaced with an ugly expression. Her fist shot out, it barely touched me as I jumped clear. It grazed my right shoulder. Don't loose your cool Karen; it won't hurt much if you stay close so she can't get a good swing. After all, that is why you chose the porch. She swung again and this time when I dodged, it went so close to my face I could feel the breeze, and connected with the door behind me.

"Ouch", she cried. "You little bitch."
NOW SHE BACKED OFF AND LOWERED HER HEAD. As she moved forward, I stepped aside and grabbed her thick hair directing her head right into the door.

"Ouch ouch, ouch" she cried as she hit the door and went down face first.

I jumped on her back and grabbed her arm, twisting it behind her.

"LET GO OF ME", she yelled. "You're hurting me."

"Are you going to pick on me any more?"

"I'll break your neck when I get up, that's what I'll do."

"Then I guess you won't get up", I said, with an amused tone. "Didn't you just swear at me? Do you promise not to hurt or humiliate me any more?" I asked, as my grip tightened on her arm.

"Yes yes, now let me up", she began to cry. My tough sister was to crying. I let her up reminding her of the promise she just made.

"I hate you, you don't fight fair", she whimpered.

"OOH, Now I wonder who I got that from? It takes one to know one."

This Old House

hy did we have to move and why would anyone want to tear down the house we had been living in? Dawn was breaking as the house came into sight. I could see the solid railing that surrounded the porch from prying eyes. I remember the rail making me feel protected from the world. It was a great place to carve on too, so anyone passing by would know there were children in this house. My favorite carving was a heart with "CL love JC" and that was to let any neighbor girls that might be interested, know he was mine.

The old house was tall and stately in the morning sun and I wanted to see it just once more before they tore it down. It had been like a beehive as the six of us kids were growing up, especially with half the neighbors kids there too. Now it was empty. It looked so old, tired, and deserted. The yard was nearly barren of grass in spite of the fact that my dad kept trying to get the grass to grow. One branch had a rope with a tire on the end tied to it where we would swing back and forth. Everyone knows you won't grow grass there, right! That made me smile. Now it's barren branches had a small cluster of leaves scattered here and there, that reminded me of tentacles on an octopus.

A demolition crew was already preparing for its destruction, so I hurried to the back. That's where the coal shed was with its steep roof covered in ugly green shingles that felt like sand paper but, perfect traction to shimmy down and drop from its low point to the ground. The slant of the roof was just right, not to steep still, a great challenge. It was worn almost smooth from the window where we came out and even our German Sheppard Ninnie joined the fun. Boy, were we dumb to think Mom and Dad didn't know what we were doing. Dad said later that he and Mom would lie in bed and listen to each of us as we made our way down the roof. Wouldn't you know, they could tell by the sound which one of us it was? After dropping down, we would race through the shed, into the bright yellow kitchen, pass the pot belly coal stove in the dining room which was by the way, the only means of heat in the house. Well, except if it was too cold then Mom would use the oven in the kitchen to help heat. Now let's see, were was I! Oh yes, then we would continue groping our way through the dark front room decorated in all shades of green. That room was only used for company. We run up the steep narrow, dark stairs and back to the window to do it all over again. Around, around, and around we went. Oh what fun it was.

The bedrooms at the top of the stairs were a trip. They were once an attic. Every time we moved around we had to be careful not to bump our head, if we were not walking in the middle of the room. In the winter when it snowed, there would be little mounds of snow in the corners of each room were it came through the cracks. The window in the front was a drop off but the window at the back of the house opened onto the coal shed roof and that's were we had our fun or you could say, our own private slide.

Whoever built this house had kept it very simple. Every room had a window and a light that hung from the center of the ceiling, including the pantry and the shed. Every room was different from the other only because of the skilled imagination of the decorator, my Mom.

Suddenly this guy yells, "Get out of the way."

A large ball crashed into the side of the house. It sounded like two cars meeting head on at a fast rate of speed. The house moaned and creaked under the menacing sphere. My heart sank as the ball hit again. The house quivered and began to fall. Clouds of gray dust mushroomed into the air. It looked like an atomic bomb had exploded taking my heart and my childhood. It was over in the blink of an eye. The dust was thick and final as I backed up to get away. It was so thick that I could taste it in my mouth and breathing was almost impossible. As I moved, I looked back at the rubble that was once my home, so full of life. Securely tucking those fond memories in my mind, down the road I go, hoping tomorrow will be as good as yesterday was.

Nightmare

It all began when I went to work for Drexal drugstore after school and on weekends. It was exciting and a great ego trip not to mention the money or the fact that Norma also came to work there. She turned out to be my best friend. We could talk openly and honestly about our deepest secrets and hopes for the future. Not to mention how good it felt at fifteen to turn my check over to mom so it could be used to help if needed. Of course, Mom put it in the bank.

I didn't like the Gordans of which Norma was the youngest. Her sister Sally left home at seventeen and never came back, not even to visit. Norma's brother Andy, didn't seem to have all his marbles and I didn't think he would ever leave. Her parents acted cold and distant even toward their children. It was obvious they didn't like children or outsiders on their property. The farm they lived on was always immaculate. There was a price to pay if anything was found out of place and the culprit could be found, if not, one of the children would be punished. Dam, even too much noise was punishable.

Take this one time for instance, her mother slapped me so hard that I fell against the cupboard because I splattered water on her wall while attempting to rinse off a dish I had been using. I wondered if that was the way people acted in the back woods mountains of Tennessee!

Norma often clashed with her mother, like the afternoon a bunch of girls decided to go over to her house after school. We got permission and all boarded the school bus that took her home. Norma's brother couldn't take us home in his old beat up truck. He said that there were too many, Norma, me, Cindy and Alice. We were laughing and talking in her bedroom when her mother burst into the bedroom and much to our horror, she slapped Norma across the face with a used monthly personal pad she had found lying in the bathroom. Norma must have been in too big a hurry to get back to us and forgot to properly dispose of it. We were so embarrassed that we promptly left the room and asked Andy to take Cindy and me home. Alice lived on the farm next to Norma so she just walked.

I was sure glad to get home that night. My Mother would never treat anyone like her Mother did. Mom liked a clean house too. She even insisted on cleaning the floors on our hands and knees so we would get the corners real clean. We didn't own a mop. Still, our house seemed to be always full of havoc with kids running in and out all the time. Mom and Dad always made anyone who came in welcome just like a part of the family. Norma spent as much time as possible at my house because of it and her parents seemed to prefer it that way.

There was one week-end I will never forget for the rest of my life. All of the girls, including Norma, spent it at my house. In my bedroom, we spent until the wee hours laughing and talking. Finally tiring, we drifted off to sleep.

I began to dream. There was fog everywhere, engulfing fields and country road. Suddenly large bulbs of light pierced the fog making eerie dancing figures as the lights grew brighter and brighter, swaying from side to side in the dense fog. Lights seemed to be coming from both directions, destined to meet. I sat up in bed rubbing my eyes. It was only a bad dream. What a relief. I lay back down, too scared to move as the dream began to reappear on the ceiling. My heart pounded as the nightmare persisted even though I was wide awake. Finally, morning came and, the bright sun shown through the window erasing the scene from the wall. Exhausted, I drifted off to sleep.

It was the week-end so Mom didn't wake us and every one slept in because they had been up late. I didn't tell anyone about my nightmare because I couldn't make any sense out of it so, you just forget it, right! WRONG, that same dream kept me awake every night for the next whole week. By the time the following weekend came I knew that I had to talk to someone about this. Norma came for the week-end and as soon as she fell asleep, it started.. I couldn't stand it any more and Norma was my best friend so tearfully I shook her until she responded, then I poured out the whole sorted nightmare.

"Candy, it's going to be all right." That's what she called me instead of Karen. "Do you know who the dream was about?" She asked as she comforted me in her arms.

"I can't tell you, I just can't tell you," I sobbed.

Funny though, having her there gave me comfort, I fell asleep without dreaming the rest of the night nor any other night after that, well at least not that dream anyway.

On the following Wednesday Norma's parents called to say they were coming to town and wanted to talk to my Mom and Dad about something, so Mom invited them for supper. They accepted the invitation. Now why would Norma's parents visit in the middle of the week? It really didn't make much sense because her father worked and her mother didn't like to travel at night. It was winter time and it got dark very early. Something was on their mind, that's for sure. Besides that, Norma came to our house after school at her parent's suggestion.

It began to get dark as we sat by the window watching for their car. Suddenly a thick fog moved in, making it impossible to see anything. Bulbs of light, in pairs, flashed occasionally through the fog. I was uneasy as it grew late and Mom decided we should eat supper before it was ruined.

"Norma, call your parents and see if they have left yet. Maybe they changed their mind", I suggested.

"Fat chance", I mumbled under my breath "Fat chance". There was no answer as the phone rang and rang. "Please Lord; let me be wrong, please."

We sat down to eat and about halfway through the meal, I bolted from the chair.

"Norma, answer the phone. It's for you."

"But Candy, the phone isn't ringing."

"Yes it is, listen." The phone began to ring. Norma looked at me inquiringly. "It's the hospital," I said.

While Norma answered the phone, I went to the closet for our coats. Dad did the driving. The eerie silence in the car was as thick as the fog around us. Norma finally spoke as we caught sight of the hospital.

"Candy, how are my parents?"

"They will both be ok," I said hesitantly.

"What else!"

"Please don't ask me to tell you more."

"I want to know the rest of your dream," Norma stated firmly.

"Your dad will die in the next five years as a result of this accident" I blurted out. "But your Mother will live a lot longer and her death will not be related. Don't ask me how I know, I just do. I wish I didn't," I sobbed. "If only I could have stopped the dream in time."

"It's not your fault, Candy," she said as we walked into the emergency entrance.

A nurse quickly scurried up to us. "Are one of you the daughter of Mr. and Mrs. Gordan?"

"I am", Norma replied.

"Then you must be Candy. Your mother has been calling for you."

"I'm Candy", I told her.

The nurse looked confused momentarily, then turned motioning for me to follow her as she led me to a room near by. Mrs. Gordan lay on a table moaning. Suddenly I was nauseated and my legs felt like jelly as I approached the bed. She looked up at me, took my hand and said, "Thank goodness you are here, I needed to talk to you, that's why we were coming tonight. It just couldn't wait. I don't want you to think this is your fault, though." Mrs. Gordan winced in pain, gripping my hand tighter. As the pain eased, she opened her eyes and went on, "Mr. Gordan and I have talked it over. We feel like you have been a good influence on Norma, in fact we like you and want you to know. Please, just don't shut us out of your lives. Back home, where we came from, it was dangerous to be friendly. People kept to themselves and run off outsiders."

She didn't know how much she was hurting me or, did she?

I was so ashamed of the way I had condemned them without knowing anything about them. I still think there is no reason for people to be mean to each other but it didn't help my guilt. After they came out of the hospital, I made it a point to make a short visit to them occasionally, but even though Norma and I remained friends, I visited as little as possible because seeing them reminded me of that night and I never could get over the feelings of guilt, that maybe, somehow it was my fault. That nightmare will live forever.

Two Houses

Let me tell you about two completely different worlds we lived in when growing up. Nothing could be more exciting than having a home in the country and in the city. Mom was the bread winner and only parent in our lives. She bought our homes when the government first began helping women to own their own home. She also became the first women foreman in the plant where she worked because of the government.

Let me tell you about our house in the city which was brand new. No one had ever lived in it. There was a bedroom for Mom and one for my two brothers and one for my sister and I. We had a kitchen, eating area, bathroom, front room and three bedrooms upstairs and a basement. We also had a big backyard. Mom had it fenced to keep the kids and dog from being hurt.

Dad wasn't allowed to come over because he was mean to everyone including Mom so we felt safe because he couldn't come over.

Back to the house. Mom let us decorate the place and it was a lot of fun. We painted the walls and arranged the furniture just right. In the basement we painted the wall to look like you were going under water as you moved down the steps. Good idea huh! We painted seaweed, fish and scuba drivers. It looked great. Everyone got a chance to paint on those walls. All the neighbor kids loved to play there and Mom had a bathroom put in so we wouldn't have to keep running up stairs. We enjoyed having the neighbor kids beg to play in our basement and it made Mom happy because she always knew where we were.

Mom got her ideas in too when she knocked out a hole in the wall between the eating area and the front room. The opening looked just like a window without glass so we could talk to people when we were in the kitchen and vice versa.

This was in Michigan and the winters were very cold but the basement actually helped keep the floors warm. The house was near schools and Mom only had to go across town to go to work. The neighborhood wasn't in the best section of town so we didn't venture far after dark and one of the reasons Mom had a fence around the property but it was a nice house and we were lucky to get it with only a mother in the house.

Now for the best part, we had an old cabin that had belonged to our Grandpa and Grandma. They sold it to us cheap. It had no running water and the toilet was an outhouse out back. Boy, was that cold in the winter and dark because there was no light in it. Mom put covers over the holes where we sat so it wouldn't smell so bad when we opened the door and hurried to get our pants down. We could get over the hole before the smell came up as the door closed. We took the toilet paper with us so it would be in good shape to use.

The cabin was north of us and they called the area Albright Shores. In the center of this community was a bridge over Wixom Lake. This lake was the center of everything, swimming, fishing, skiing and winter carnivals right on the frozen ice. This place was so small it didn't have street lights or paved roads or police unless, one was called from the near by town which happened sometimes if someone got hurt or drowned in the lake. Now this was freedom. Grandpa bought us all motorbikes and we could tear through the area without worry about breaking rules like it was in the city.

We got our water from the neighbors well. Bugs would get in that old shack, even snakes so we decided to build a house on the lot next to it which was part of the property Mom bought from Grandpa and Grandma. And build we did. It had running water, septic and shower all in the house. It became harder and harder to go back to the city when the weekends were over so we decided to move to our new cabin and rent or sell the house in the city.

It was hard for Mom though because she had to travel a long way to get to work. She did it for us. We hopped a school bus that came through our area on its way to the nearby town called Beaverton. Mom traveled 100 miles a day to work and back plus she worked a lot of overtime. She would leave early in the morning and come home after dark.

We were alone a lot but one thing Mom always insisted on was that we ate together and always check in regularly. The neighbors kind of looked after us.

Sometimes we missed her a lot when we needed someone to talk to and sometimes she was so tired that we didn't think she heard what we were saying anyway. Those times were hard for everyone. I wonder which you would choose, if you had to choose; the city or the country life?

Who Needs Parents?

Mark Allen, you are 17 and free. All you have to do is climb on that bus and you can do whatever you want or be anything you want to be - at last.

I looked over at my sister Karen who had come to the bus terminal to see me off. She was timid and shy and had been so dependent on me over the years that I felt pain and a twinge of guilt at leaving her behind. I reached into my pocket and took out the letter from Dad to re-read in an effort to prolong saying our good-byes.

My mind drifted back to the day everything changed for me and my world came crashing down, I came home from school to find Karen huddled in Mom's arms at the kitchen table. Dad was sitting at the opposite end of the table.

"Mark," Dad said, "Your Mother and I have something to tell you."

Mom interrupted, "Your dad and I have decided not to live together anymore." Your father has accepted a promotion and is being transferred to Texas which is a long way from Michigan.

Dad quickly interjected, "But I will come to see you and Karen when I can and write to you often."

"But Dad, I can't read writing yet and why are you going?"

He half smiled and lowered his head, "My work has kept me traveling and away a lot so you'll hardly notice and besides, I can call you on the telephone and maybe I can take you both with me sometimes."

I liked Dad because he was always laughing and playing games with us when he was home. As a traveling salesman, he always brought something good home for us when he returned. Even though he was gone far more then he was home, I still didn't want him to leave.

He finally stood up after a long silence, kissed Karen's cheek, walked over to me with a sad smile, ruffled the hair on top my head, picked up his suitcase by the door and walked out quietly closing it behind him, without looking back.

"Why is Dad going away Mom?"

"He needs some space, I guess?"

"What space, Mom?"

"I can't explain now but someday you will be able to understand when you are older."

After that Mom went to work selling real estate. Mom wasn't home much and we rarely heard from Dad, it seems he was just too busy to spend much time on us. Karen and I grew into our teens with one babysitter after another. None of them seemed to please Mom or us either, for that matter. One babysitter even locked us out of the house all the time while she entertained her friends. By the time I was thirteen, Mom was fed up with the sitters and decided I was old enough to take care of Karen and myself. That was the end of my growing social life. I couldn't have friends in the house without Mom there and there was no spending the night at a friend's house either.

Mom and Dad were always too busy to come to any of our school activities. I tried my best to be at any events Karen was in at school and she was always there for me because I wouldn't leave her by herself.

Dad would call and say, "Son, are you taking good care of your Mom and Sister!" I guess that made me the man of the house. Mom left a list of chores for us every morning that kept us busy.

Karen was such a baby and sometimes it was so irritating to have her follow me around, hanging onto my shirttail, that I would yell at her, then she would start crying and I had to put my arms around her, tell her I was sorry for yelling at her and reassure her that I loved her. Karen loved to play house and of course, she played the mother. I think for this reason she learned to cook and clean just like a pro. I would say she was better than Mom but then Mom didn't practice much anymore. Mom did however, make a good inspector.

I would go to bed at night and dream about doing things like the other guys. Here I was in my teens and hadn't even had the chance to hang out or do any of the things they talked about at school. If it weren't for Karen, I would have run away several times.

I was so lonely at home that I buried myself in homework to alleviate the boredom. I didn't realize it then but it paid off with a college scholarship. Dad was delighted and agreed to pay anything the scholarship didn't cover.

Today was the big day, and I was ready with my bus ticket in hand. As usual, Mom wasn't there to see me off because she had an important house closing. Dad covered as usual by sending me a letter to wish me luck, the letter also included a lecture on keeping my grades up and my nose clean. His last words were, "Son, make me proud. Love ya, Dad."

I snapped back to the present when Karen said, "Mark, I think your bus is getting ready to leave." There were tears in her eyes. I hugged and kissed her, vowing to write often. Now where had I heard that before! I quickly turned and boarded the bus so she would not see the tears in my eyes. Somehow this scene had a familiar ring to it from long ago. Choosing the nearest window, I waved goodbye. I could see that she was turning into a beauty and knew she would be all right because, after all, I raised her and did a pretty good job, if I do say so myself.

As the bus pulled away, I couldn't help thinking about the price others pay for our actions or how these actions affect our lives. I only know that I can not stay as I am and I hunger to expand my world, so with an ache in my heart and butterflies in my stomach, the bus moves forward into a new life. Maybe this was the way it was for Dad! Is this what Mom meant by needing space? Maybe, but I think there must be more to it then that, more determined then ever to be better and closer to my own family when the time comes.

What Happened to George?

Me and my pals George, Ronald, Skip, and Punky grew up in Beaverton, Michigan. I liked it there. There were no cops and living was lazy. Lots of poverty, but we didn't care. My girl friend Mary, best friend George and I all graduated from Beaverton High this last June. George and I promptly got jobs where our fathers worked.

George bought a station wagon with the help of his Dad so we could cruise around on the week-ends. And one Saturday night, he went to a rock concert in near by Flint with some of the guys where he worked. He called me the next day after church.

"Listen Wink," he said, all excited, "I met these far out girls at the rock concert last night and they invited me to a party at their house in Flint this Saturday night. The girls want me to bring more guys and spend the night. We haven't had a party since my 17th birthday except, for our graduation so, it's time for another one. How about it? You wanna go? I'm gonna ask Ronald, Skip and Punky too.

"Gosh George, I don't know!" You know Mary and Mom, will never let me go to a party where there are girls and leave her at home, especially to a big city like Flint."

"Aw, come on, you're old enough to make your own decisions besides, Flint maybe bigger than our hick town but it's no Detroit, you know. Come on Wink, you have to break away from Mom's apron strings sometime. Look, if it makes you feel better, tell your

Mom you're going to a concert and will spend the night with me, at a friends in Flint, because the concert will let out too late, OK?"

"What about Mary?" I repeated.

"What a bummer, Wink. So, take Mary and I'll take my new girl friend Barb to keep her company, since they already know each other. I don't know if the girls will let us in. I think they just wanted guys, but we can give it a try. We can all meet at the bridge in town, at 7:00 o'clock Saturday night, Ok?"

"Okay, George, I'll be there if Mary will go."

Saturday night sure came fast. Mary and I reached the bridge and saw the whole gang there, George, Barb, Skip, Ronald and Punky. We all piled into George's car and headed for Flint, a good hundred miles from Beaverton. George assured us that his old "Vista Cruiser" as it was called, would make it there and back with ease.

The house was not hard to find but when Rosie answered the door, you could tell she was not real happy to see that we had brought girls. It turned out to be about two girls to every boy. It was Rosie's party and she was the one who had invited George. These girls had beer and they were dishing it out even to us, and of course, we weren't 21 yet. She kept watching us and after the second beer, she decided to ask us to leave. We, or at least I wasn't used to drinking and I didn't feel real good. The party wasn't getting off the ground and I'm not sure why Rosie invited us anyway but I suspect they were up to no good.

George and his brother, Ronald seemed to be the only ones not affected by the beer. George decided to drive. He got behind the wheel, turned on the radio loud and rolled down the windows. It was November and cold. Ronald took the front passenger seat and the rest of us squeezed into the back seat. Good thing it was a station wagon because there was more room behind the seat if someone wanted to lay down. George's brother Ronald was the oldest. He went a lot of places with us and usually kept an eye on things. We pretty much, listened to him. On the other hand, Punky was also their brother but, being the youngest, no one listened to him. He always tagged along every where.

I soon dozed off into a light sleep. I don't know how long it was before I realized the car had stopped and was parked along the highway 175. I looked around. Ronald and George were getting out of the car. It looked like George was going to let Ronald drive. George disappeared around the back of the car and Ronald went around the front. It had begun to snow and the pavement was wet. Very bright lights shined through the rear window as a car approached from behind. Just as the boys were to the front and rear of the car, there was a sound of squealing tires followed by crunching metal as the car we were in, was hit from behind. The impact threw me forward as the car lurched forward and slid sideways toward the ditch. My head began to spin as everything went black.

I don't know how long I was out but somewhere in the dark, I could hear sirens and voices near by. I don't remember getting out of the car but suddenly found myself running down the middle of the road toward on coming lights. There were cars and people in clusters near by.

Someone must have called the police and in the distance the sound of an ambulance could be heard. A hand reached out and grabbed me, pulling me toward the side of the road and in the direction of the car which was now lying on its' side in the ditch.

It was Punky pulling on me. "Help me find George, the last time I saw him he was at the back of the car where it was hit and now he's gone. He has to be somewhere around."

Ronald was leaning against the car, holding his leg. He had been thrown onto the hood of the car with the impact. "Are you all right, Ronald?"

"Jesus, Wink, I have a deep gash in my leg. I can't stop the bleeding."

"Squeeze it and Hang in there, help is on the way. I can hear sirens. I'm going to try and find everyone else."

"Hey Wink, I saw Skip sitting on the ground at the rear of the wagon. He looked pretty beat up. I think, he must be hurt too. The rest are looking for George! He probably got tossed somewhere when the other car hit because he was standing where our car was hit. I hear sirens. Who called? Did you?"

"No maybe someone had a cell phone," I said. "I was knocked out and right now I have a headache that is so bad I can hardly see straight. Did you see Mary or Barb?"

"No. That car must have been traveling pretty fast to hit us that hard.

"Hold on Ronald, I'm going to try and find George and the girls before the ambulance gets here" I shouted..

Just passed the car, Barb came into view. She was sitting at the top of the ditch with her knees up and her elbows resting on her knees.

"Are you all right Barb? Where is Mary?"

"Yes, and Mary is looking for George in the field."

Mary called, "George, where are you George!" A wave of pain shot through her back by her kidneys. Mary knew she was in trouble; she had just got out of the hospital with kidney problems not over a month ago. She staggered forward, "George, answer me, where are you?"

I reached Mary and as I grabbed her hand, we both heard George's voice directly ahead, barely audible, "Help, help me someone, I can't move my leg."

We found George, and Mary stayed with him while I headed back toward the car, to get help. The ambulance and police lights could now be seen as they pierced the night sky, there lights spinning around and around in splashes of red and blue. As I came closer, I could see Ronald and Skip being put into the ambulance. Punky and Barb kept pointing into the field as they stood talking to the police. They saw me coming and I signaled them to follow me. I could hear another ambulance in the distance. They caught up to me as I reached George and Mary.

"Three more ambulances are on the way, hang in there," one of them announced as they reached the three of us.

There were two people in the other car and the driver was a man who had fallen asleep at the wheel, according to what we had found out later. There were four ambulances and they took all nine of us to the hospital, including the people in the other car.

George only had bumps, bruises and a broken hip which the doctors said could be nicely repaired without difficulty because George was young and healthy. Skip also had some broken bones so the two of them were kept at the hospital. The rest of us were treated and released. Mary was told to see her doctor because she had bruised kidneys and they were swollen. I had a mild concussion and Ronald was also released after they sewed up his leg. God was sure with us that night and I give thanks for that. George's father came to the hospital and took us all home while George's mother remained. His father then returned to the hospital.

It wasn't until the next day that I told Mom everything and asked her to take me back to the hospital to be with George. I knew he going to have surgery on his hip. This is what happens when you let the devil sucker you into doing what you know is not right. If I had only listened to the voice inside me. Mom didn't lecture me thank God, I was already hurting enough. She just took me to the hospital.

George was anxiously waiting for me. "Wink," he said, I saw Jesus in the field where I was thrown, last night. He told me to make peace with everyone, set affairs in order because he was coming for me, soon. Wink, I'm scared. When Mom and Dad comes today, I need to have them bring the minister. Will you tell them to hurry?! Tell them to come right now; I need to talk to them right now. Please Wink, will you call them right now! Ask them to get a hold of the minister and see how soon he can come. It needs to be before the surgery because I won't be coming back."

"Sure George, I'll do anything you ask but don't be silly, the doctor said you're strong, young and healthy so there is no reason why you shouldn't come through the operation with flying colors. I think you were just hallucinating from shock."

"Well, I'm wide awake now Wink and I know Jesus was there."

Even though I didn't really believe him, I did what he asked. Later that day the minister came. George talked to him for a long time behind closed doors. When the minister finally came from the room he told us there was no doubt in his mind that George was telling the truth about seeing a vision. George also convinced his parents but, somehow I just couldn't believe it. After talking to them, he seemed happy, joking and laughing with us. He seemed just like his old self in spite of the injury. He smiled at me and said, "Everything is OK now".

Before surgery the following day, the gang gathered around his bed to wish him luck and assure him that we would all be waiting when he came out of surgery. "Hang in there man," we all yelled as they wheeled him down the hall toward the operating room. He waved back with a big grin on his face and his eyes closed as his hand dropped down to the table.

Five hours later the doctor emerged from the operation room to tell George's parents and the rest of us, that all had gone well and he was in the recovery room. "His vital signs were good throughout the surgery," said the doctor.

Suddenly from the loud speaker came the call, "Doctor Ingels to recovery, **stat**". The doctor turned immediately, excused himself and rushed back through the doors from which he had appeared. We all stood there, not knowing what was going on nor what to do next. We were all still standing around waiting when about ten minutes later the doctor returned. He looked grave and somewhat disoriented as he approached us again. "Mr. and Mrs. Smith, I can't explain it and I can not see a medical reason for it at this time but your son stopped breathing and we were unable to bring him back. I'm so sorry to have to tell you this." Mr. and Mrs. Smith thanked him, turned around and just walked away without saying a word.

I phoned Mom right away, fighting back the tears. "Mom, George didn't make it. I hurt so bad, I just want to go home". It didn't matter if the whole world saw me cry, I just lost my best friend. How could this be?

George was buried in a little graveyard by the bridge in town were we spent so many hours together. He would have wanted it that way. George was born January 18, 1957 and died November 11, 1975, at the age of 18. I guess God really did come for him. Maybe he is the lucky one, to make peace with everyone that mattered here and then to join our Lord and Savior. I will always be grateful for the time I had with my friend George. Sometimes I still think about how his parents quietly accepted his death. We are all here for a time already determined; providing we don't do something to rush it. Guess I'll always wonder what George told the minister and his parents to make them believe or to except what happened with peace in their hearts. Surely Jesus touched George's parents and relieved their sorrow.

Three Sisters

Donna, Joy and I are sisters as different as day and night. No one would guess unless they knew the family, that we were even related. Donna had long very dark hair and dark complexion with medium bone structure, a stem look and serious personality. Now, Joy on the other hand was big boned, blonde, light complexion and bubbling with personality. However, Donna and Joy had something about them that was appealing and both were about the same height. Donna had this quiet voice that hinted of hardness while Joy had a loud husky voice that burst like a trumpet with commanding charm. It is hard to say which one has had the most hardship or heartbreak in each of their lives. Donna seemed to take everything in stride with quiet determination while Joy carried everything on the surface. Both of them had a great passion for people, surrounding themselves with family and children.

Sometimes I would look at Donna and sense her great depth unshared by the world. It could be intimidating and uncomfortable even though she was younger than me. She could listen to your woes and show no sympathy but Joy however, would rarely listen because she was too busy talking. She could make you laugh and make you forget your troubles. Joy ended up divorced after three children. I suspect she was being abused. Donna however, accepted her marriage and coped with it come what may. She was always a strong person. Donna had dropped out of school to get married while Joy graduated and didn't marry until she was twenty two. Now I know you're going to ask where I fit in since alluding to the fact that there are three sisters here. I was the oldest of us three with nothing in common and no close relationship. I was neither outgoing nor shy, neither good looking nor ugly. You might have called me a Nerd but I'd say I was just me.

A Price to Pay

It was 7:00 a.m., the whistle was blowing and the sound of machinery pierced the air. A new day had begun but the routine is the same, day in and day out. It didn't take brains to do these jobs, just dexterity so my mind constantly wandered into hopes for the future or recalling pieces of the past.

This day, for some reason thoughts of the past began to crowd my mind. It started with the memory of an old house where wind whistled through the cracks and snow filtered in with it to form small mounds in the corners of the room. There were two bedrooms upstairs, one for the boys and one for the girls. Mom and Dad's bedroom was downstairs off the dining room. There, sitting smack dab in the middle of the floor was the pot belly stove heating the whole house. We had a coal shed attached to the back of the house to keep that stove from going out. Needless to say, it was warmest in that dining room and the bedrooms up stairs were the coldest.

I lay close to my two sisters Joy and Donna, to keep warm and made sure the covers were over us. While waiting for everyone to fall asleep, car lights entertained me by making eerie figures across the wall through a window facing the busy street below. I didn't like the room because those figures always seem to be alive. It was a relief when everyone was asleep and I could sneak down stairs to lay my covers by the stove and stay toasty warm. Besides, it was next to my parent's bedroom. So comforting.

The stairs were dark and some of the boards creaked so it was very important to feel ones way carefully so you wouldn't fall or cause a loud creak. Now to get through the front room without tripping over furniture in the dark was the last obstacle. The doorway to their room was close to the stove and instead of a door there was only a drape, so one had to be QUIET. In the morning, Mom would step over me, bending down to kiss my cheek as she headed for the kitchen to pack our school lunches and make breakfast before going to work.

Once we were awake, she would leave for work and not return until well after dark. There were six of us and it took both parents to support us, especially since they never turned anyone down who was in need, child or adult. Our home was always open. Probably because Mom grew up in an orphanage and Dad had to quit school after the 7th grade to support 5 sisters and his mother and father. His father was disabled and his mother ill. She had something called dropsy!

They always looked so tired and it seemed like everyone in the world needed something from them so it was hard to get their attention. I would have liked to tell them how much I loved them but I didn't.

Dad was strong and he made me feel safe. He was also the kind of person that attracted a crowd. He had a soft side too. I remember the time he gave the brand new jacket he got for Christmas to a ragged old stranger who had on just a tee-shirt for a top and it was very cold outside. When Mom asked why he did that, he said, "That poor man had no coat and I have many in my closet at home".

Mom was very different from dad. She was hard working, patient, had a strong sense of duty to her family and above all no sense of humor. You could tell a joke and at the end, she would still be waiting for the punch line. Some how, the time never seemed right to take any of my problems to them when so many people were ahead of me.

Back to what I was trying to say, things didn't seem right as I made my way down the stairs and through the dining room. The kitchen light was on and it shone dimly into the dining room. Strange sounds were coming to my ears. It sounded like crying. Cautiously peeking around the corner, I caught sight of my Father. He was sitting at the table with his head in his hands, slumped over. He WAS crying. I couldn't believe it. What happened? What could be so terrible that it would make my Dad cry? Then the door opened, and closed. It was my Mother's voice shrill and angry.

"I don't love you any more. Do you hear me? I don't love you any more."

It's a good thing it was dark so they never knew I was there. Back in my room, I cried.

The next day was as though nothing had happened and the night before was only a bad dream. I couldn't believe my Mother could do something like that to my Dad. It was so cruel. I would never do anything like that to my husband or my Dad. I would never forget that night even though it was something they kept from their children and every one else.

I was only sixteen when I met my future husband. He was five years older than me and I was flattered by all the attention he was giving me. He was handsome and just out of the Army. I had almost no experience with boys. Being lonely and very plain was not exactly the type of girl boys chased. Being introverted and shy with long dishwater hair, weighing seventy nine pounds soaking wet was not exactly what most boys were looking to be seen with. He followed me every where and wanted to be with me all the time. He asked me to marry him.

This was my chance to prove myself to my parents and to the world how a good marriage works and to make them proud of me. Besides, I loved him and he loved me. Mom and Dad didn't say much. She just looked more tired than usual, but Dad cried.

He put his arms around me and said "I love you baby".

I felt so bad, what had I done. It was too late to take it all back and for the second time; two people he loved made my Dad cry. Some how I hope to make it up to him with a grandchild and a good marriage. Little did I know that a sixteen year old didn't have the wisdom to deal with life yet.

There was something wrong with Robert's need to control and dominate. My parents knew that better than me and feared for my future. They were so right. He was cruel from the beginning and I was his property. Robert kept me from my parents for fear that they would influence me. He didn't understand, I didn't want them to know.

For the first five years I was pregnant with one child after the other. After four children and a miscarriage, there could be no more babies. For twelve years, he abused the children and myself, so with a great deal of courage and fear, we were divorced. Working was not unusual because Robert had never worked during our marriage. He was too busy keeping track of me. If one incident by Mom and Dad impressed me so much, then I wonder what will happen to my children as they grow up with all this pain and suffering. I pray for them every day and will always be there for them.

There goes the whistle, time for lunch, thank goodness for a break from those thoughts. They need to remain in yesterdays memories as lessons for tomorrow.

Theobald's Theory

There I sat in my communications class, staring at the pile of stapled paper. The title "The Background to the Guaranteed Income Concept", stared back at me. The thought of reading another dull chapter on economics followed by an equally dull report of the chapter depressed me.

I was only half aware of the author's works until Mrs. Beckwith said he was one of the radicals of our time. If Robert Theobald was a radical, I wanted to read his chapter, and then I could put him in his proper category with the rest of the nuts.

I plunged into the chapter with one thought in mind, to get this assignment over with.

Theobald was convinced that his theory would give everyone a guaranteed income. To do this; society would have to be oriented to unemployment being just as good as employment. Truly, a radical change from being raised to believe work is good and idleness is bad.

My self, I figured Theobald's Theory would work for the aged, disabled, or to subsidize students, but the healthy people of this country would feel like they were getting a handout. That's my theory, of course. It leans toward socialism and away from capitalism.

Theobald stated that the reason we find ourselves in economic problems today is not due to our past failures but because we have progressed with automation to the extent that we need less people to labor. If everyone was guaranteed-income, people would seek a more meaningful activity and then would take turns with the limited labor tasks.

Sounds like a tour of duty in the armed services, if you ask me.

His theory had a great deal of logic and understanding of peoples desires. It hit home with me because I hated my tedious job, but it put food on the table. The time could be better spent with my children. Also, there would be time for the things I would like to do. His theory had some good points.

Theobald also reminds us society is already working toward his theory by instituting sick pay, unemployment benefits, paid vacation holiday pay, etcetera. At some point we would have more time off with pay then work time with pay.

We have technology to produce goods and services with little or no human contact right now, such as our cybernetic plants.

It occurred to me that people have pride and ambition. They seem to want to out do the guy next door. People also have a strong need to control. How would that affect Theobald's theory? I took his theory to work and asked my co-workers. To my surprise, most of the girls were ready for the idea, a suggestion was made to start a crusade for guaranteed-income. The idea of pursuing more desirable interests and making use of untapped talent was exciting to them. No one stopped to question what level the guaranteed-income would be established at or how this type of income would be administered.

I concluded the idea was not irrational if it could make a more satisfied society without killing the incentive to be productive. In my opinion, Robert Theobald was ahead of his time. Our society may embrace his theory in the future but those thoughts are still in their infancy, although we may be fast moving in that direction.

The Morning After

There was a phone ringing, first in my subconscious, then in reality. Startled, I jumped out of bed.

The first recollection of the night before came in spasms of pain stretching the entire length and width of my head. The room was spinning as my shaking hands reached out for support from the night stand, fighting to bring the room into proper perspective. The phone continued ringing in harsh monotones. I looked up at the clock and strained to read it through the blurring maze; seven fifty-five. With great effort I reached the phone, fighting off waves of nausea.

"Hello!"

"This is Thelma from work, are you sick Sandra?"

"No, I'm sorry; I must have overslept. Thanks for calling. I'll be there as soon as possible, bye."

My throat was parched and a thousand percussion instruments were beating in my head. At the sink, I swallowed a large glass of water with several aspirin. It entered my stomach like cold water thrown on a hot grill, I headed for the bathroom.

Turning on the light switch was like the flashbulb of a camera. It took a few seconds for my eyes to accept the light. Standing before the mirror was the image of a person I didn't recognize from the day before. Where was the glowing hair, sparkling eyes, smooth rosy checks and sweet smile? This image reminded me of Phyllis Dillar with bloodshot eyes. Putting on make up and covering my eyes with dark glasses helped a little.

The aspirin was finally taking hold and within a few minutes the old Sandra appeared, at least on the outside. My stomach still reminded me of what not to do when one has to work the next day. In the car, I popped several mints into my mouth in hopes that no one would get too close. It's a good thing birthdays only come once a year so there will not be another surprise party like that from my friends any time soon. This promises to be a long day.

Hello Chicago – Hello Airplane

Ed Duby, our local union president approached.

"Carol, there's a special meeting in Chicago and I can't get away so, as vice president you are next in line to go."

"Ok Ed, but do you know this will be my first time ever to fly?"

"No I didn't. It will be a good experience for you, not just in flying but in what is expected of you, if you are elected president as I think you will."

The arrangements were made but as the time grew near, tension and fear took hold. My stomach was queasy, legs rubbery, dizzy and generally ill all over. I began to itch, leaving red streaks all over my body. It was now or never as I charged through the gate like a bull to his death. It was first class for me while everyone else seemed to be going to the back of the plane. The first class seemed to be on the empty side and I wondered why? The stewardess began to speak from the loud speaker, she didn't sound scared at all. If she could do the flying for a living, surely I could get to Chicago and back. As the plane took off into the sky prickly heat took hold of my body and it became hard to breath. Soon the no-smoking sign went off and the stewardess asked if I would like to drink. Not much of a drinker, I hesitated.

Looking around I asked "what does mostly everyone drink?"

The stewardess said, "Martinis."

"I'll have one of those too, please?"

Mixing the two bottles that came with the glass, I took a sip. It tasted awful. This drink tasted like rubbing alcohol but, it did change my whole perspective. Off came the shoes as I relaxed, so much so that there seemed to be a little difficulty controlling my movements. Even my attitude changed. It wasn't so bad up here, how dumb to worry.

It seems as though we just went up and we were coming down already. The stewardess was giving her farewell speech and it was time to get off the plane.

My legs were unsteady as I stepped into this large airport. What now Carol? Follow the signs, they point downstairs to get a cab. Both feet were moving, one in front of the other but it seemed like I was walking on air.

"Taxi driver take me to the Ascot Hotel."

"Where's that, in Chicago?"

"Of course it is in Chicago, right inside the loop. Don't you know your city?" Of all the cab drivers, I had to get an idiot. It was an uncomfortable feeling. Feeling superior, I stared at this crude man with his filthy cab and opened a window to share the stale odor inside with the rest of the world. He spoke to me with an air of disrespect for my superior position. We finally reached the Ascot and it was such a relief to get out of the cab and away from that driver.

"That'll be $7.50 lady."

Pulling a wad of bills from my pocket, I tossed one at him and turned abruptly calling over my shoulder, "keep the change." Before I could pick up the luggage sitting in the middle of the sidewalk, the cab driver swept it up with a grin showing large white teeth and headed through the hotel doors.

"Come on lady, I'll take care of these for you."

What could have changed his attitude? He wasn't going to get away with that. "Put those bags down." He set the bags down and without saying anything, left. It really was out of character for me to act like that; I didn't know what the matter with me was. The desk clerk gave me a room key and I paid for the room in advance. As the money was counted, there appeared to be $10 missing but maybe I just miscounted.

At the elevator a short, middle aged man stepped forward blocking the way. "Who are you?" he asked looking me over with an amused smile.

"Who are you?"

"I'm a comedian" he retorted.

"To bull you are, you're a bartender."

Astonished, he asked, "How did you know I was a bartender?"

"I guess I know one when I see one."

"Are you coming into the bar to have a drink?"

"Give me time to get settled first, ok?"

It was two in the afternoon, the meeting wasn't until seven so after showering and a change of clothes, I decided to go to the bar. The bartender was delighted to see me. Not wanting to mix drinks, I ordered a dry Martini and sipped it slowly as we talked about nothing important. He bought me a drink and then went back to work. Someone sat down beside me and ordered a drink for me too. Beside me was sitting a tall, thin well dressed man. He smiled.

"I'm an income tax investigator and you?"

"Just here for a meeting," I mumbled sliding off the stool and wished the door wasn't so far away.

Inside my room, I collapsed on the bed. I looked at the clock. That was the last thing I remember, 4 o'clock.

I woke with a start---the clock---quarter after seven---can hardly move---must get to the meeting---good thing it's in the building. I took a cold shower, dressed and made it to the meeting at seven forty five. Bill Crucher grabbed me in the doorway and led the way to the nearest chair.

"Where have you been?" Got the word you were coming and was assigned to be your escort."

"Fell asleep and just woke up, sorry."

There was a lot of business to be transacted which lasted that evening and all the next day. Somehow, I got through it all. I managed to get through it in spite of the way I felt. It was as though I had been drinking the whole time or drugged but it was neither.

I was escorted to the plane and got safely aboard even though the plane ride back was only a blur. I had started to cough constantly. The stewardess felt so sorry for me, that she kept feeding me soda.

Ed met me at the airport, took one look at me and asked if I wanted him to take me to the doctor. I said that I did.

The doctor said it was walking pneumonia but that it was almost gone. It was so good to be home and on my way to my own bed.

One thing though, Ed told me Chicago Union called and said I handled the job well and they were very impressed. A good end.

A Mother Knows

The pains started after scrubbing Mom's floor on my hands and knees. I took a deep breath and doubled over, falling against the kitchen stove. There had been no warning. What could be wrong?

Just then Mom entered the kitchen, took one look at me and knew something was wrong. "What is it Karen?"

"I don't know Mom except it feels like labor and the doctor just told me two weeks ago that I was not pregnant."

"Allen, come here quickly," Mom shouted.

Another pain hit and my knees buckled just as Allen entered the kitchen.

"You better get Karen to the doctor right away" Mom cried.

Allen was my husband. He promptly took a hold of me and escorted me to the car. Helping me inside, he pointed the car in the direction of the doctors' office.

"Allen, please don't take me like this. Let me go home and get cleaned up. My knees are dirty, hair messed and my cloths and body smell of sweat."

He looked over at me and hesitated, "Are you sure?"

"Yes, please Allen."

He swung the car around and headed in the direction of home.

Every time a pain hit, I fought to keep from letting it show. Finally we were home. Each time there was pain as I climbed the stairs to the bathroom, meant a delay until it stopped. The pressure became so great it seemed as though some foreign object was trying to open the door to freedom from inside me.

The pain was eased but the pressure was mounting. For some unexplained reason, I grabbed a towel, put it on the floor and squatted over it instead of sitting on the toilet. Well, maybe in the back of my mind, I knew the doctor was wrong. A warm bulky sensation came over me and I could feel myself open to release a soft mass of flesh that fell into the towel which was being held barely off the floor. The mass fell so gracefully to freedom.

"Oh my God," I screamed. "It's a baby. I've just had a baby. How can this be?"

Allen came running up the stairs and took the baby, already turning blue, wrapping it up in the towel and disappeared with it in his arms.

I sat staring at the floor where it had just been laying. None of it seemed real. Allen returned, lifted me from the floor and helped me down the stairs and back into the car.

"It's going to be alright Karen. It's going to be alright", he soothed. We headed for the doctors office.

The office was filled with people. We entered with me screaming and sobbing, "My baby I lost my baby." The nurse quickly appeared and rushed me to a back room. A needle penetrated my arm and my feet were strapped in the air. The doctor starred in total disbelief until Allen laid the baby on his desk. Upon examination, there had been no signs that a baby was ever there, not even bleeding. But, the proof was on his desk. I lost my child forever.

Twenty-Four Hours with My Grandson

Last night I took my one year old grandson home for the weekend. Today it seemed as though I hadn't slept all night. My beautiful bright blue eyed, strawberry blonde, chubby grandson slept with me. He tossed and turned in his sleep and ended sleeping horizontally across the bed. It was almost impossible to keep covers on and most of the night was spent shivering.

My eyes opened reluctantly as a hand slapped my stomach, not so gently and a voice echoing "wet Granma, wet". I slid from the bed to my feet with my wet grandson, under one arm. It probably wouldn't be wise to know why Wayne had that big grin on his face when he had a diaper so wet it spilled out onto his outer clothes. Wayne was a hand full but after washing him up, a changed diaper and clean clothes, we finally made it to the kitchen to prepare breakfast. It was an experience to watch him eat by the spoonful. Bacon, eggs, toast, milk, and oatmeal disappeared like a garbage disposal. I understood why the family nicknamed him "Drano".

From the time he came until the time he departed, the house was a disaster area. Cupboard doors were open with their contents spilled out and lying mostly anywhere in the house. Toys were everywhere.

Every weekend I would tell myself that Wayne was not going to come this week. But every Friday, I would stop to see him before going home. Those sparkling eyes, happy smile and outstretched arms would greet me and I would melt. Here I go again.

On this one particular visit, Wayne was at my feet with his arms wrapped firmly around my leg while I was trying to cook. There was a fresh cup of coffee sitting on the table and I longed to drink it in peace and quiet. Besides, it was dangerous for him to be at my feet when I was using the stove. I reached down and pulled him off.

"Go in the other room and play with your toys Wayne," I commanded A stern look told him I meant business.

He turned to leave showing his displeasure and I went back to my cooking. Suddenly, there was a crash and I swung around to see my cup of coffee lying on the floor. It's contents had spilled all over Wayne. He looked up at me with wide eyes and his mouth open. For a few seconds I just stood staring until Wayne's expression changed and he began to cry. His face turned red and distorted in pain. There was a blood curdling scream. I grabbed him and removed his shirt and pants. The whole front of him was red as a beet from his chest to his legs. I just happened to have medication in the bathroom for bums which was applied liberally.

I just let him run around naked the rest of the day, applying medicine periodically. He sure loved not having clothes on and I sure didn't like cleaning up the puddles he left behind. By evening, the burn had been reduced to a red spot about the size of a silver dollar on his tummy, thank heavens. Darnedest thing was that the coffee was all down the front of him except the private area. There was a big round white circle in the middle of all that bum. This time I really will let him stay home for a weekend.

———

About the Author

CAROL J. ALLEN

Born: August 4, 1937 in Saginaw. Michigan. U.S.A
Oldest of six children
Married and raised four children, David, Carol Ann, Wayne and Sandra
Married second time in 1978 to William H. Allen with one step daughter Stephanie
Eleven grand children and 10 great-grand children
Two years college (Labor Relations)
Two years "Institute of Children's Literature"
Writing and painting began in junior high school
Poems published in the "International Library of Poetry"
"The Best Poems and Poets of 2007",
"Collected Wispers" in 2008
Also served on several over seas mission trips.
Currently Reside in Houston Texas.